Zoom! Zoom!

written by Pam Holden
illustrated by Jim Storey

Look how fast
I can go on my
skateboard.

Look how fast I
can go on my bike.

4

Look how fast
I can go on the
water-slide.

Look how fast
I can go on my
skates.

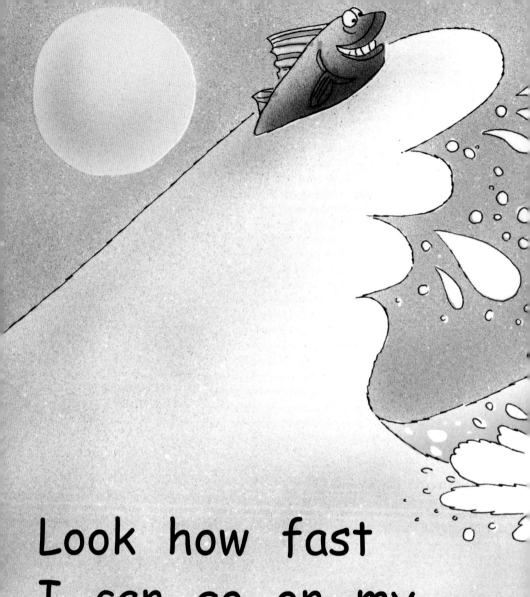

Look how fast
I can go on my
surfboard.

Look how fast
I can go on my
scooter.

Look how fast I
can go on my skis.

Look how fast —
Ooops!